The Adventures of Granny Clearwater & Little Critter

To my grandfather Henry Mitchell and to the loving memory of
my grandparents J. P. Mitchell, Howard Willis, and Zora Willis
—K. W. H.

To Mrs. Murphy, who taught me how to celebrate life with
generosity, wackiness, and strength
—L. H. B.

Henry Holt and Company, LLC, *Publishers since 1866*
175 Fifth Avenue, New York, New York 10010
www.HenryHoltKids.com

Henry Holt® is a registered trademark of Henry Holt and Company, LLC.
Text copyright © 2010 by Kimberly Willis Holt
Illustrations copyright © 2010 by Laura Huliska-Beith
All rights reserved.
Distributed in Canada by H. B. Fenn and Company Ltd.

Library of Congress Cataloging-in-Publication Data
Holt, Kimberly Willis.
The adventures of Granny Clearwater and Little Critter / by Kimberly Willis Holt ;
illustrated by Laura Huliska-Beith. — 1st ed.
p.   cm.
"Christy Ottaviano Books."
Summary: As the Clearwaters travel west, fearless Granny and Little Critter are jolted from the horse-drawn
wagon and have many exotic adventures before being reunited with the rest of their family.
ISBN 978-0-8050-7899-2
[1. Adventure and adventurers—Fiction. 2. Grandmothers—Fiction.
3. West (U.S.)—Fiction. 4. Tall tales.] I. Huliska-Beith, Laura, ill. II. Title.
PZ7.H74023Ad 2010   [E]—dc22   2009027418

First Edition—2010 / Designed by April Ward
The artist used fabric scraps, stitchery, paper, acrylics, and computer collage to create the illustrations for this book.
Printed in June 2010 in China by South China Printing Company Ltd., Dongguan City, Guangdong Province, on acid-free paper. ∞

1 3 5 7 9 10 8 6 4 2

The Adventures of Granny Clearwater

& Little Critter

Kimberly Willis Holt

illustrated by Laura Huliska-Beith

Christy Ottaviano Books

HENRY HOLT AND COMPANY ❀ NEW YORK

ONE DAY

the Clearwater family decided to head out to where the sun sets—that place called the West. With Ma by his side, Pa drove the wagon. The older Clearwater children walked while Little Critter and Granny rode in the back.

For miles and miles the land was as flat as Ma Clearwater's burnt corncakes, but all of a sudden the wagon hit a big

HOLE.

Pa snapped the reins extra hard and those horses commenced to running. The jolt was so rough that Granny and Little Critter shot out of the wagon like cannonballs.

They flew through the sky for almost a mile until they landed stuck to a prickly pear cactus. Granny kept napping as if nothing had happened, but Little Critter's eyes popped wide as he watched his family's wagon disappear from the horizon.

When Granny awoke and noticed their predicament, she swung loose of the cactus needles snagging her blouse. Then she pulled Little Critter from the cactus with one swift yank.

Little Critter's behind looked like a

Granny plucked each needle and rubbed some prickly pear juice over the bumps.

Sizing up the situation, Granny said, "We'll stay put so your pa can find us." Then she remembered—ever since Pa got hit on the head during a cow pie toss, he'd confused north, south, east, and west.

"Well," said Granny, "sooner or later we're bound to find them."

Each day Granny and Little Critter walked across that leave-your-mouth-scorching-dry prairie heading west. They got so thirsty Granny had to do a rainwater dance taught to her by her grandpappy with itchy feet. Why that desert had never seen such a downpour.

They became so hungry they could have eaten Granny's boots. Instead they ate fried prickly pear cooked over mesquite.

FINALLY, trees replaced cactus and mesquite. Granny and Little Critter got a hankering for something more than fried prickly pear. So when they came to a lake, their tongues went to hanging like a half-starved hound dog's. Granny snapped two limbs off a tree, pulled the thread from her skirt hem, and bent two hairpins into hooks. Then she showed Little Critter how to dig for

WORMS

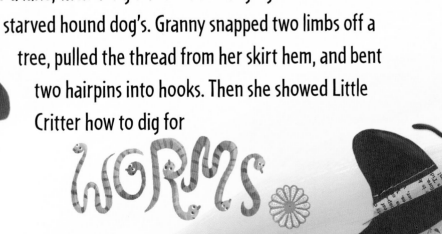

Soon they were dipping their lines into the lake.

Every time Little Critter felt a tug, it turned out to be nothing more than a turtle nibbling. But Granny—now that gal could fish. She'd learned how years ago from her ma. Granny caught one trout after another.

And when a fish pulled so hard that it dragged Granny into the water, she kept aholding on. The fish took Granny around and around the lake until it wore plumb out. Then Granny swam to the bank, pulling the fish behind her. That night they ate until their bellies swelled as big as melons.

ARCTIC CIRCLE

When they'd been gone a spell, Little Critter pointed to something **HUMONGOUS** shooting up through the clouds. It was taller than a giant and wider than a thousand women wearing hoop skirts.

"Yonder is a

One Hoop Skirt = 1 Jillion Miles

said Granny.
"We'll have to cross it."

During their journey they stumbled across
a sign posted on a tree. Granny read aloud so
that Little Critter could understand.

Granny Clearwater frowned at the man's picture.
"He's uglier than a mud fence," she said. "And I never
could stand a bad poet."

Two days passed when Granny and
Little Critter heard a lady

A second later, they saw what all the commotion was about. A man with a rose between his teeth was holding up a stagecoach. Every person stood outside with arms pointed toward heaven.

Granny took off her stockings—all seventeen pairs. Little Critter pulled off his stockings, too. Granny tied them together and swung them above her head. She'd learned to lasso from her Grandma Coleen when she was just a wee tot about the same age as Little Critter. All the women in her family could handle a rope pert near as good as a snake charmer handles a rattler.

The stockings sailed through the air and spun faster than a windmill on a windy day.

Just as the folks were about to hand over their money and jewelry, Granny's lasso slipped over Rose Rogers' head and slid past his belt buckle until it reached his knees. Then Granny gave the rope one strong tug.

ALASKAN
TERRITORY
(WAAAYYY
BeFoRe Alaska
was a state)

CHINA

AUSTRALIA

Rose Rogers fell to the ground before you could say

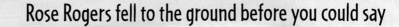

The folks cheered.

Flat on his back, Rose Rogers began to recite:

Oh wisp of a woman with gray hair
Her roping talent is surely a scare.

Little Critter didn't particularly take kindly to bad poetry either so he crawled over to Rose Rogers and bit one of his ankles. That shut him up all right.

Granny and Little Critter rode in the stagecoach. When
they arrived at town, the sheriff threw Rose Rogers in jail
and presented the reward money to Granny and Little
Critter. He even named them honorary deputies.

When Granny told him they were trying to meet up with
the family out West, the sheriff gave them his quickest pony.

It seemed like everybody in that little town wanted to send a letter to someone heading west.

With all the mail they had to carry, there was barely room for Little Critter.

Granny jiggled the reins and that pony took
off like a pebble snapped by a slingshot.

They crossed the

MOUNTAIN,

then made their way through a

VALLEY, stopping only long enough
to deliver the letters. Why, you'd never seen such a Pony Express.
All the time they kept their eyes peeled for the rest of the Clearwater
family. But they didn't see hide nor hair of them. Finally they reached
the West and stopped at a place called California.

A bunch of folks out there were panning for gold. Years ago Granny's great-uncle Corky had shared his panning secrets with her. So with Little Critter by her side, she picked a spot upstream and heated her frying pan over the water.

That frying pan grew so hot it dried up the stream and melted the gold nuggets into a beautiful liquid that flowed down smooth as syrup into Granny's bucket.

PA's Shortcut
NORTH POLE
ARCTIC CIRCLE
ALASKAN TERRITORY
NORTH AMERICA
ASIA
MAP
INDONE
PACIFIC OCEAN
AUSTRALIA

One day when Little Critter was making mud pies, he heard a whistle that sounded familiar, though he couldn't rightly say why. He looked way off to where the land and the sky touched and noticed a wagon. He ran to fetch his granny. She could spot a mosquito landing on a fence post a mile away.

"That's your **Ma** and **PA!**" she shouted.

Sure enough it was. Ma and Pa and the other Clearwater children took turns squeezing Little Critter. A few months had passed since they'd seen him last and they'd missed him something fierce.

"How'd you find us?" asked Granny.

"Well," Pa said, "I took a shortcut. I knew we'd meet up sooner or later."

"It looks like it's time for a  " said Granny.

Her aunt Carlene had taught her a thing or two about using a hammer and a saw, and that day Granny passed those tips down to the rest of her family. The Clearwaters began to build their home like a mess of busy ants forming a hill. Even Little Critter helped.

When their home was finished, Granny plucked a banjo she'd learned to play from her pa. Little Critter banged a spoon on the bottom of an old kettle. Everyone else danced until the sun sank low in the sky and they'd worn holes in their STOCKINGS.

The Clearwater family had finally settled out West together!

AUTHOR'S NOTES

"Pert near" means almost!

Pardner, this here tale has been stretched from one end to the other pert near like taffy. However, a few pure-d facts inspired these pages. If you want a spitting view, then just hold on to your saddle and take a look below:

"Pure-d" means authentic!

WESTERN MIGRATION

Between 1815 and 1840, people migrated west of the Appalachian Mountains. Since wagons were filled with supplies, most women and children walked the entire journey following their family's wagon. The railroad transformed the country, offering another option to travel.

The majority of railroad building took place in the 1850s. In a decade, the nation's tracks increased from 8,879 miles to 30,626 miles, more than enough to circle the globe.

Are we there yet?

THE GOLD RUSH

The gold rush began in 1849. Word spread, and the next year eighty thousand people traveled to California from all over the world. Those first gold seekers were called "forty-niners."

STAGECOACH ROBBERIES

Stagecoaches were used as a mode of transportation throughout the mid and late nineteenth century. However, robberies became more common after Wells Fargo started using stagecoaches to transport money. In the 1870s and '80s, one robber, a man known as Black Bart, was finally caught. A few of his trademarks were that he used polite language while robbing his victims and sometimes left behind a printed poem.

My request is not so little:

GIVE ME ALL YOUR PEANUT BRITTLE!

Neighbors often helped a family of newcomers build their home. This was also a type of social entertainment. While the men worked raising the house, the children played together and the women spread a dinner on the ground.

THE PONY EXPRESS

From April 1860 to October 1861, young riders rode fast horses, carrying letters in as quickly as ten days from St. Joseph, Missouri, to Sacramento, California. This method of delivery ended with the introduction of the telegraph.

PEANUT BRITTLE

Peanut brittle was originally called groundnut candy. Recipes can be found dating as far back as 1847.

GRANDPAPPY

AUNT LOU

AUNT MILLIE

AUNT BETTY

GREAT-UNCLE CORKY

GRANDMA COLEEN

AUNT CARLENE

MA

PA

LITTLE GRANNY